FOR: ZACH

May your

Hunter's "Quest"

Be FILLED with Big (DEER) RACKS + LOTS of Great history!

Mara Mae
2014

HISTORY CPR
CULTIVATE
PRESERVE
READY

Thank you.

Written by Mara Mae
Illustrated by Dan Smith
Layout by Sandy Sharp

First Printing May 2014

Copyright © 2014 Mara Mae

ISBN 978-0-9915655-0-4

Printed in Michigan

Published by Old Wood Press
P. O. Box 777
Ironwood, MI 49938
www.historyprize.org

Acknowledgements

Thanks to my kids and sisters who continue to support my love of the fine arts, and my endeavors as a writer. Sincere gratitude to my new "family of friends" in Ironwood-Hurley, who have expressed their kindness. Thanks to those who took my heavy pack, or carried me through the chapters of this book as I overcame many challenges while writing this story. Much like Hunter, I drew a lot of happiness from being with friends. Not one friend, old or new, is ever taken for granted. With Love, MM

Thanks to the incredible people at Heritage Guitars for your unending passion to bring handcrafted, quality instruments to the world. Sincere appreciation to Scott Makohn and the folks at Shakespeare's Pub. Thanks to the excellent people at the Michigan Historical Society who have further improved the History CPR book series. Sincere appreciation to Ironwood and Hurley Public Schools for introducing History Prize to students during the Pure Michigan Governor's Conference. Thanks to Michigan History magazine as you continue to bring history to the page in ways that ignite the imagination. Special thanks to John Thomas for his excellent work in highlighting the place of women in the Gibson WWII history. Gratitude to Kalamazoo River Valley Museum. Enormous thanks for the social studies and art educators at Kalamazoo Public Schools (KPS) along with special thanks to: Principal Greg Socha who supported History CPR (2011-present) and to many of the terrific KPS teachers and members who have been critical to my success in developing Hunter's Quest: Heather Morrison, Julie Davis, Jackie Denaway, Doug Duncan, Kathy Murphy, Ellen Williams-Bierline, Julie Ermingtinger, Julie Scott, Chad Jansheski,

Tony Wine, Katie Kay, Yonee Kuiphoff, Kate Kemmerling, and Donna Judd. Enormous thanks to Kalamazoo Public Library. Special thanks to Larry Peterson for his diligent efforts to create a heritatge tourism network and for his support of fellow writers and illustrators. Sincere appreciation to Dean Margaret Hauck who worked diligently to bring History CPR to Michigan residents and lift Kalamazoo through her Creative Endeavors program at the historic Michigan News Agency. Thanks to Roxanne Coleman and Shakespeare Company. Roxanne, your enthusiasm for fishing, history and the outdoors was an inspiration to me on this project! Thanks to Sandy Sharp. Sandy, in so many ways and on this book project, you helped me sail above deadlines and demands. I look forward to creating more great products and services with you!

From the Illustrator:

Thank you to my wife, Laura, for being a patient hand model, tireless cheerleader, and loving muse. Mudbug and Kevlar, you were more help than you know. Thank you to my big, wonderful family of brothers, sisters, cousins, nieces, nephews, in-laws, and outlaws for their unending interest and assistance. Chloe, Brie, and Lexie were some of my models, Alisa my consultant. Thanks also to my Kincheloe Elementary School compatriots for their belief that an old principal can do anything. Patti Wiggins and Diana Flanders, you helped me sprout. Kristi Wagner and Tara Fletcher, you were terrific. Thank you to the many dedicated teachers and principals elsewhere that boosted me up and were anxious to help. Eric Cardwell and Roger Moore, for instance, should be cloned. Tom Neale and Janet Manos, I sure owe you one. Thank you to my friends, Karen Hardisty, plus Bill and Janice Klinesteker, for ceaseless encouragement. Steve Barber, I appreciate the strong insight and clear vision that was generously given. And thank you to all the children and students that launched me on my way.

Dedicated to:

Gibson and Heritage Guitars
Employees and Luthiers
1902 - Present
&
Shakespeare Company
Employees and Lure Artists
1897 - Present

Table of Contents

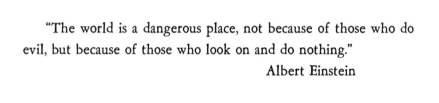

"The world is a dangerous place, not because of those who do evil, but because of those who look on and do nothing."

Albert Einstein

1

Questions

Why did my family move away from Ohio in the middle of my best Little League season? How can I be in Kalamazoo, Michigan for six months and it feels like ten days?

When I came to Kalamazoo, we moved into a small suburb called Oshtemo. Oshtemo is a township located about 30 minutes from Lake Michigan. I feel at home when I'm at the lake and so far, Lake Michigan has been my favorite place to spend time. Our home however, even after months, doesn't feel like home to me. My old bedroom had three big windows and lots of nooks and crannies to hide stuff. I knew every inch of my bedroom in Ohio. I guess it's because I lived there since I was born. This room seems different. It is bigger and I lose things, important things. I can't even remember where I hid my candy box from last year's Christmas stocking. It's been missing since I unpacked. To this day, I can't find it. When will this house or this bedroom feel like home? Our house in Ohio felt like home to me. Will Kalamazoo ever seem the same? It's not just the house we are in. It's the whole place. I mean really, how did my parents manage to find a neighborhood, in a city with more than 75,000 people, where every house is occupied by girls? I am not kidding. On my street there are six girls and three of them come over all the time: Sophia, Emma, and Abigail. Further down my

Vintage Lake Michigan from author's collection.

street: Sierra, Chloe and Cassie. Almost ten girls in a 1-mile area! I am practically the only boy living in Meadow Farms. "Meadow Farms" is what they call this neighborhood. In Meadow Farms, it feels like girls and dolls are everywhere. Questions! That is what this move has given me: an endless line of questions!

Starting with questions, what about Michigan snow storms in April? Who has snow on Easter Sunday? We were supposed to visit my Uncle Scott's place in the Upper Peninsula (U.P.) and the car ride from Kalamazoo to Houghton is over 10 hours! I was up for the long ride. I wanted to see Uncle Scott. He is one of the most interesting people I know. Yet, we were snowed out of our spring break trip to the U.P. since they had a small blizzard. A blizzard in April? Where Uncle Scott lives in Copper Country, they had 300 inches of snow last year! The weekend we were supposed to be there for "spring break" the whole West U.P. was dumped on with 10 inches in one day! Uncle Scott said cars were being pulled out of snowbanks left and right. Of course, we had to postpone our trip to the Upper Peninsula. Moving to Michigan has brought me an endless line of questions! Haylee, on the other hand--she has answers. Plus, Haylee has lots of new friends. She has a favorite math teacher and a great cross-country coach. I'm sure it will be the same when we go back to school this fall. For Haylee, moving to Kalamazoo has seemed peachy. For me: questions!

Kalamazoo Ladies Library Association c. 1879

2

A Place of Promise

Did I tell you the whole reason we moved here? Initially, it was to be closer to Grandpa Joe and Grandma Ann. They are getting older, and my parents had always talked about moving back to Michigan to be closer to them. I didn't think it would ever happen, but when Mom got a call for an interview in Kalamazoo, and a few days later a job offer, plans started to fall like dominoes. I was shocked and I hate to admit this, but I felt like crying that first night when Mom and Dad told Haylee and me we were moving. Haylee did cry, and that was stressful too. Here's what I remember from that long and difficult night.

Mom said, "The country is still coming out of a recession."

"Ohio is one of the hardest hit states, a number of people have lost their jobs, and businesses are recovering slowly..." Dad said.

"Can't you get another job?" I asked.

"I could, but we would still need to relocate, Hunter. Some businesses are cutting back on travel, especially flights. I have no choice, Hunter, we have to move. I will be able to find more work as a pilot," he said.

I could see where they were coming from, but it didn't make the move easier. My parents were leaning toward Kalamazoo. On top of the "job thing," Kalamazoo had something no other city in the United States of America had. It's called "The Promise" or in my words, "the clincher." Try talking your mom out of free college for two kids. Here's how they explained The Promise. "If you two go to school in Kalamazoo, your college tuition can be paid for," Mom said.

"What do you mean?" Haylee asked.

"It means that you and your brother could go to any Michigan college and you don't have to pay for college tuition at all. You can just attend, and not worry about student loans for tuition," Mom said.

Dad pulled a napkin out of the napkin holder, and started drawing on it. He drew the bottom part of Michigan that looks like a mitten. Then, he marked an X on the map where our home is located in Ohio. From the X, he drew a line up to Kalamazoo. As the conversation continued, we talked about the Universities scattered around Michigan and with a red pen, he marked each of them with a star.

"Any of these Universities--plus Northern Michigan and Michigan Tech in the U.P.--any of these public universities starred would be eligible," he said.

"We can attend for free, if we just move there and graduate from any Kalamazoo high school?"

"Yes," Mom and Dad replied in unison.

It looked like a million miles from Ohio to me.

"All you have to do is graduate," Dad said, convincingly.

"With reasonably good grades," Mom added.

With The Promise in mind, my mom and dad had no second thoughts about moving to Kalamazoo. I can't say the same for me, but I'll tell you again, the best part of moving has been Grandpa Joe!

You have to meet him. He will be coming over soon! Sometimes, he just sneaks me a dollar when Mom's not looking, and then we travel around together, not to boring places, but to interesting stops. If I even look bored he asks, "What's next?"

Gibson Guitar Factory, Kalamazoo, Michigan 1941

3
On Parson Street

Would you think after six months in Meadow Farms it would be easy to have friends by now? It has not been that simple. Easier said than done, the idea of making new friends. With school starting soon, I have to get used to the idea that Gramps and I have only Saturdays and holidays together through the school year. Gramps shows up here every Saturday at 8 a.m. and we leave my house. Usually, we start by going to the Victorian Bakery where Gramps will read the paper and talk to bakers while having a cup of coffee. As he's chatting, I get to pick out pastries, and by the time we leave, we have an enormous box of baked goods--soon to be devoured! We deliver them to the guys at the guitar factory on Parson street.

The factory is called Heritage Guitars, and it is located in the old Gibson Guitar building. The first thing you notice is a massive smoke stack, and when you walk in, there are tall, wavy glass windows. The building has creaky floors and a very distinctive smell. "An old-time smell" breathes through the walls and around corners of the building. Everywhere on the factory floor there is a dusty but magical feeling. Most of the luthiers work at the factory all week, but they don't always show up Saturdays. When they do, I get to watch them and help them polish off their guitars. From what I can tell, making a guitar is about carefully turning pieces

of wood into the shape and body of a guitar, and getting all the parts working the way they are supposed to. Luthiers make ordinary pieces of wood into valuable guitars. My grandpa knows a lot about the process, because he started making guitars in 1952. When he retired in 2005, he had been making guitars in the same building for over 50 years!

"If you think about it, this is an art form," Gramps explained.

"Guitars become a source of sound that changes lives and people," one of the luthiers tells me.

When Ren, my favorite luthier, makes a guitar he will sometimes explain what he is doing to the guitar. Today, Ren is making a guitar top.

"There we go," he says, brushing off the wood. "I will make my cut now, and yes, that should be just about perfect."

He turns away from me, and I watch him set the piece of wood into a miter saw. He told me all about the miter saw last weekend. After he makes some careful adjustments and runs the saw, he holds the wood up, proudly.

"Look at that feather edge! Now, I have everything cut for the shooting board, and we have what we need. So with the parts waiting for us, we can get to marking things. Next, measurements!" he says. "Go ahead, mark this," Ren chirps.

Ren points to a specific place on the piece of wood he has been working on, and I pick up a pencil and mark the edge. "Good, that helps us remember where the edge will sit. Glue time!" he says, smiling.

"Can I help, Ren?" I ask.

"Of course! We have to make a nice, tight joint now," he says, holding up the guitar. "I think the guitars turn out better for me when you come in and help."

"I love coming here and watching you make guitars, Ren."

"Maybe someday, you will make guitars here too," he says.

"That would be great!"

Truth is, I wouldn't mind working at the factory someday. I like watching Ren and the other luthiers at Heritage make guitars. I want to learn how to play the guitar too, except it seems when I play, I get annoyed with my fingers. My fingers don't act right on the strings and my mind and fingers don't want to work together. On the other hand, when I grab a bat, my fingers are very happy, so I don't know if I'm supposed to play guitar or swing a bat. Gramps plays guitar, and he tells me not to give up. He tells me to keep practicing on the guitar. He claims if I don't quit, my fingers will catch on. He says playing guitar starts with getting your fingers used to the strings. Ren walks back in and blows the dust off the top of the guitar again and runs his hand across the guitar body.

"We want this ramp to be smooth. The ramp needs to clear the wooden edge, nicely," he says.

He keeps working, and talking me through the whole process, as Gramps walks over to where we're standing. I know Gramps will start wondering if I'm getting bored, but I'm not. I like watching Ren make guitars. All of us stand around the table working on the guitar together. Gramps holds a piece of wood for Ren. As they work together, adjusting pieces of wood on the guitar, they take off on little side stories about some of the people who used to work at Gibson or about guitars in general.

"I'll pop a couple of nails in," Ren says.

He takes the nail gun and shoots the nail into the wood.

Nail guns make a cool sound," I say.

"She's a handy gadget," Ren says.

Almost every Saturday night, Gramps and I meet with whoever wants to come out and play guitar, and sometimes that includes the Heritage luthiers. We always seem to end up downtown at Shakespeare's Pub, where the owners let us play around and usually we take up a back corner of the restaurant. When Kalamazoo musicians start showing up, someone will usually find a microphone and sometimes people walk up and start singing, as if they were on stage. By the end of the night, favorite songs are played and shared histories of special guitars have been told.

Many of the Gibson guitars, made at the Kalamazoo factory, eventually became famous! On days like this, Gramps will tell me about famous people he met when Heritage was Gibson. Gramps happens to be one of five guys who stayed back in Kalamazoo, when Gibson Guitars decided to move to Tennessee. Now, internationally famous, the Gibson guitar company has headquarters in Nashville, but Gibson Guitars had their earliest beginnings in Kalamazoo!

I think that is pretty cool. The other fascinating part of Gibson and Heritage history is that sometimes famous people will buy one of these guitars, play it, and fall in love with it. Maybe one of the guitars I've seen being built or that I put a bead of glue on could end up being played by someone famous!

The most famous electric guitar in the entire world is named Lucy. The reason I know about Lucy is because one Saturday morning Bill, a luthier, was making a guitar at the factory. He was telling me why they named the cats at the factory Lucy and Strings. "Of course, Strings is obvious," he said.

"But we named Lucy after George Harrison's famous red guitar. At one time, that guitar had been stolen, and after many years of searching it was finally recovered, and returned to the famous musician. Lucy remained with him until he passed away," Ren said.

As we walk into the factory on Parson Street, I imagine luthiers pumping out five hundred guitars a day, like they had at the factory a long time ago. I like knowing all of the history, not just because it is part of my own family history, but because it is part of America's history too.

4

Girls and Guitars

Ren starts to work on a part of the fret board on a second guitar, but he keeps talking the entire time.

"There used to be 1,000 people working in this building, and the place was buzzing and still the best sound was simple tuning and strumming to see how the guitars were working," Ren says.

I have learned a ton of things about Gibson guitars. Orville Gibson made unique flat-backed mandolins at the Gibson factory in 1902. Ren tells me Gibson had to wiggle through the difficult WWII years with a lack of resources.

"Everything had to go to the war effort because the manufacturing of 'luxury items' like guitars had to be put on hold. In spite of wartime challenges, Gibson put out 25,000 guitars during WWII. The factory didn't advertise much during the war, but guitars were still being created at Gibson. Mostly, Gibson advertised 'repairs' on existing instruments. Making new instruments had to be toned down during war time," Ren explains.

"How did they make guitars when all of the guys were in the war?" I ask.

"We had a lot of young ladies that became excellent luthiers during those years, and some of them even returned to join the huge boom of guitar making that occurred at the factory when the war ended," Ren says. "Young women came in and worked the string room, and did some of the intricate hand work like adding inlay pieces onto the guitar necks. Women would sand and polish guitars, and sometimes we lost them for awhile because they would leave the factory to go see their boyfriends or spouses who went 'on leave' from the war, and then they would return when their boys went back to the front lines."

"Sounds like Gibson might not have made it through the war without girls in the factory," I reply.

"The gals who built guitars during the war were very important. They kept things going at Gibson, and in other factories around the country too," he says.

"Do you think Gibson would have shut down without women?"

"I'm not sure, but I don't think they could have managed without them very well, since most men were fighting in the war, and women worked hard back at home. In those years, the decal on the guitars said 'Only a Gibson is Good Enough,' and you have to admit, that claim was built by the hands of women who were making sure Gibson guitars were truly quality, great sounding instruments," Ren says.

"Who was the most famous person to use a Gibson?" I ask.

Ren smiles, "Do you mean my favorite or the most famous?"

"Both."

"I guess my favorite and one of the most famous too was a gentleman named Woodie Gutherie. He played his famous song 'This Land is Your Land' on a Banner Southerner Jumbo that was made right here in Kalamazoo," he says, proudly.

"Buddy Holly was famous too, and many other famous musicians came up with great hits on Gibson guitars, but I still love thinking about the magical tunes that Woody made. He loved to strum his guitar from Kalamazoo," he says, dreamily.

"Did anyone famous ever come to the factory?"

"Oh sure, sometimes they even played a little concert here before they left with their new instrument, and those were the highlights after the hours of tedious work that went into making those famous guitars," Ren says.

Luthier at Gibson Guitar Factory 1936

5

A Doll in Kalamazoo

During the school year, Gramps says we will keep making bakery runs to Heritage on Saturdays. I love that we bring in breakfast for everyone at Heritage on the weekend! I would miss it, if we stopped. I love seeing who comes to play or "chuck around the wood" as Gramps would say. You never know who will be at the factory on Saturdays. It could be Zeke, Brad or Sarah; it could be Bill or Ren. It's hard to say who will show up, since they work all week too and Saturdays are extra hours. After Heritage and whatever else Gramps and I do, I come home on Saturdays to do my chores by late afternoon. Then, our house starts to fill with girls. There are girls in the basement, and if not there they hang out on the patio, or in the back yard, or in our tree house. Sometimes they do hair and nails upstairs in Haylee's room. From what I can see, Zumi is Haylee's best girl friend. I have to admit Zumi is actually a pretty great person, and I like her easygoing way. Mom calls Zumi a "positive force" and I have to agree. You cannot help but like Zumi, so I'm happy for Haylee to have a friend like her.

Zumi's family moved to the United States from Nigeria. Zumi and her family have a unique way of saying English words and I love listening to her, and the distinctive way she accents her words when she is speaking to you. When we lived in Ohio, we didn't have as many neighbors. We didn't have people from such different backgrounds and cultures. I had lived there so long that I had a bunch of friends from school. They would always come over. Haylee had friends there too, but it seems like Haylee has many more friends in Kalamazoo. Before we moved, Haylee played with me a lot. Now, our days of building Legos, and running through the back fields behind the house in Ohio are distant, fond memories. Here I watch Haylee play with her friends. All summer it has been dolls, dolls, dolls! Mom made dolls for Haylee and Zumi the first month after we moved in. All of this girl-doll time is kind of hard for me to take. Mom doesn't realize how tired I am of defending both sides in games, and building Legos isn't quite the same without Haylee. At least there's Gramps! I love the sound of Grandpa's truck pulling into our driveway. Usually, he brings Lindy with him. As soon as they arrive I can see them from my window, I can see Gramps tossing Lindy her stick. Gramps talks about how high Lindy jumps. I agree, Lindy can jump so high. She can jump higher than any dog I know! To survive girls and dolls in Kalamazoo, I need Lindy and Gramps to get me through!

Bronson Park, Kalamazoo, Michigan c. 1900

6

Half-a-Chance

I have one major problem that needs sorting out before school starts. I am not sure what to do about this kid on the other side of our neighborhood. His name is Chance. He's the only boy I know in Meadow Farms, and he can't seem to be nice to me. Actually, I think Chance is a bully. It started when Chance and I had a rocky first encounter. Lots of girls were at our house, and that day Chance decided he would see exactly what was going on in our yard. Our yard, as often was the case, was filled with five or six girls. I walked out of the house that day, and I saw Chance showing off his Tae Kwon Do moves for the girls. He appeared to be absorbed in their attention. I walked slowly down the drive and hoped to get by him without being noticed. I wasn't that lucky.

"Hey, Hunter, right?" he asked.

"Yup, that's me," I said.

"Come on, help me out with this," he hollered.

I made the mistake of listening. I turned and walked to the group of observing girls. Next, he asked, "Can I do some moves on you, Hunter, you know just to show the girls a few defense tactics?" he said.

"Nah, I don't think so," I said.

"Oh come on what are you, chicken?"

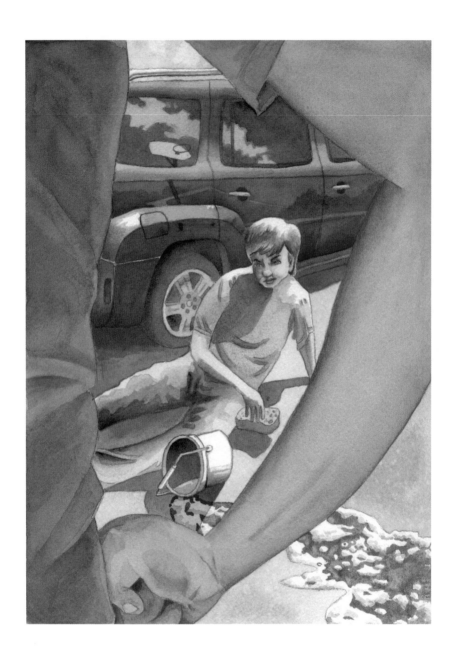

I started to walk away.

"Chicken Little, Chicky-chicky-chick, come on, it won't hurt-- I'll take it easy," he jabbed.

As I walked away, Chance shouted every chicken name I had ever heard in my life. I felt a little better about things when all of the girls left Chance standing alone in the yard. It doesn't take too long before everyone sees a bully and my sister is pretty good about this sort of thing. Haylee doesn't "do bullies" and it seems her friends are the same way.

I might have given Chance a new half-chance, but I had no idea where to begin when I saw him after that first day. I couldn't help it, I felt lesser than him when he looked at me. I hated those feelings. Even though it wasn't true, I knew he wasn't better than me or anyone else. The next disaster with Chance came when I was washing Mom's car. I went to the house to get more towels, and when I returned, all of the soap buckets had been flipped upside down. At the end of the drive, Chance was standing there, laughing and pointing at me. Worse yet, he was with two boys I had never seen before in Meadow Farms.

"All washed up, hey, Hunt?"

"Keep on scrubbin', Bubbles," another boy said.

After that, I ended the idea of ever having any great friends (who were boys) in my neighborhood at Meadow Farms. I mean, the only three that were my age, and who lived close enough to play with me, were not the kind of kids I felt I wanted to get know.

To get my mind off of Chance, I decide to ask Mom to bring me out to Grandpa's. Grandma Ann and Grandpa Joe live right next to Kal-Haven trail. Maybe Gramps will be up for taking a bike ride. By the time we make it out to Gramps' place it's getting dark. I find Gramps standing in his workshop in the warm light of his old lantern. Gramps is sorting through fishing lures in his garage, and with lures on his mind, fishing is sure to be part of my weekend.

"Here's the one!" he says. "I remember catching the biggest sunny on this, out at Wolf Lake, last June," he remembers, proudly.

"So, what have your mom and dad been up to?" Gramps asks.

"They've been busy with work, and the yard. Mom has been putting a new exhibit together at the museum, she's been getting home late," I reply.

"Did your dad say if he would be joining us for the Kal-Haven bike ride this fall?"

"No, probably not. Maybe next year he said, when I asked him."

"I guess Catherine has something for him to do, hey?" Gramps asks.

"I guess," I reply.

"Does that disappoint you a little?" Gramps asks.

"Kind of, but we're still unpacking and getting settled, so eventually I think Dad will start doing stuff with me again," I say.

"Until then, you have to put up with me," he says, winking.

"Oh, Gramps, it's fun, I only wish I had a friend my age who could come with us," I reply.

"That would be nice, wouldn't it?"

"Yes, I would love it! So far it's only Chance, and we don't get along."

"Chance lives at Meadow Farms?" he asks.

"Yep, but he's a bully," I say.

"Why is that?" he asks.

"He is a real jerk," I say.

"Is there anything good about him?"

"Not sure, I haven't found anything yet," I say. I pause for a minute. "I don't know if I'll ever know the answer to that."

"Well, should we find out the answer?" Gramps says.

"How do we do that?"

"Let's go over to his place and maybe we can meet him," Gramps says.

"Really?" I say, in disbelief.

"We could discover Kalamazoo together and in the meantime, we'll see if there is anything good about Chance," he says.

"Good luck," I say, rolling my eyes.

"I'm curious, I never met a Chance before. Now's my chance," he says, elbowing me with a wink.

"Hey, where did you get this one?" I ask, holding up a lure.

"Your mom won that lure, in a kid's fishing contest, but I've been keeping it safe for her, hoping soon I'll have a chance to take her out fishing; since you live closer, I bet I can!"

"You have a zillion lures, Gramps."

"I do have a fair collection. I started to collect lures at about your age, and I kind of look for them now, especially Shakespeare."

"Why Shakespeare?"

"Well, they had a factory here, just like Gibson, they started in Kalamazoo about a hundred years ago and then, when they became really big they moved. But when I think of Shakespeare rod and reels, and of course these lures, they're all from Kalamazoo, originally."

7
Summer's Best Two Weeks

The usual routine of waiting for Gramps starts with a round of basketball in my driveway when an unexpected beeping begins and keeps on going. It's coming from a huge moving truck backing into the driveway across the street. It jolts my thoughts at first. The house where the truck is backing in has been empty since we moved here. At the blue house, several people are talking. Some are moving items from a moving van to the house. Out of the house walks a girl. Great, another girl, I think. I go back to shooting hoops and trying to ignore the ruckus. The next thing I know, there's a noise coming up the driveway.

"Tatump, Tatump, Tatump!"

The echo of a second basketball shoots up my feet and into hands. I spin around. I see a boy about my height, and definitely my age. He has a huge smile. I am not quite sure I will ever forget that moment. Nope, I am pretty sure I can't forget. It's the first time I met Nevin. Nevin has a huge grin that goes ear-to-ear. His big brown eyes are just staring at me with a "ready to play" shine.

"Want to shoot some?" he asks.

"Sure, I do," I say, feeling a little stunned.

"My name is Nevin."

"I'm Hunter," I reply.

"Good to meet you!"

Of course we only have a few minutes before Gramps pulls into the driveway.

"Just a minute," I say.

"Okay," Nevin replies and keeps shooting.

"I'll be right back."

I run down to Grandpa's truck.

"Hey, Gramps, I met a friend,"

"You did?"

"Yup, his name is Nevin and his family moved in next door".

"Wow, isn't that great?" he says, smiling.

"I'll be right back," I reply.

I run back to Nevin, while Grandpa parks his truck.

"Hey, are you going to live here for awhile?" I ask Nevin.

"Yes, I think we'll be here for a long time," Nevin says.

Those words are sweet music to my ears. Gramps must have been reading my mind. He walks up the drive and puts his hand out to shake Nevin's hand.

"Hi, I'm Grandpa Joe and this is my dog, Lindy" he says.

"Hi, I'm Nevin, it's nice to meet you, and you" he says, patting Lindy's head.

"Do you think you might want to go fishing with us?" Gramps asks.

"Sure, but I don't have a pole or fishing tackle," Nevin replies.

"That's okay, we have extras. What do you think your parents will say about you fishing since you are just moving in today?"

"Oh, that's probably nothing, I am supposed to stay out of the way of the movers," Nevin replies.

"Great then, let's go meet your parents, and see what they think about you catching some fish," Gramps says.

We walk toward the moving truck and when Nevin's dad sees us, he comes over and shakes Grandpa Joe's hand. I hear them talking and smiling and the only stinky thing that occurs is this awful feeling that sweeps over me. I have a feeling we're being watched. Sure enough! In the corner of Nevin's backyard I catch a glimpse of Chance. He's glaring at us. There's a quick feeling of terror inside my chest. What if Chance wrecks the moment? I pray no one notices Chance, and that he won't have any time to mess things up. Happily, and before I know it, Nevin, Grandpa and I are sitting in Grandpa's truck and riding to Wolf Lake!

At Wolf Lake, Gramps pulls our bikes out of the back of the truck. We start out biking around the hatchery ponds. They are several small lakes and ponds that provide different habitats and are used in different ways. On the ledge of the first pond there are turtles basking in the sunshine, ignoring us and clearly soaking up the warmth of the day.

"Every time I come here I see something new or interesting," I tell Nevin.

"When we first came out, right after we moved to Kalamazoo, the baby sturgeon were jumping in the main pond, it looked like it was raining on the pond as minnows flipped up and out of the water everywhere," I explain.

"Wow, I want to see that someday!" Nevin says.

We spend the morning fishing and in the afternoon Grandpa surprises us both and takes us to the *Gilmore Car Museum*!

I have never been to the *Gilmore Car Museum*, and of course Nevin has not been there either. It's the best Kalamazoo day so far!

Driving back to Meadow Farms I know with the time we have left before we go back to school, this will be summer's best two weeks! Grandpa and Nevin chat all the way home, and I don't think I can quit smiling.

"One day we will visit the *Air Zoo*," Grandpa says.

"What's the *Air Zoo*?" Nevin asks.

"Oh it's a pretty neat place where air flight history is kept and explored."

"Sounds interesting," Nevin replies.

"Nevin, what do you like to do in your free time?" Grandpa asks.

"I play basketball, piano, and I take guitar lessons. I play video games too," he adds.

I can't believe my ears. Video games, basketball, guitars!

It's great that Gramps is asking these questions, since I'm not sure I can speak with my mouth stuck on smile.

"Hmmm, we have friends at a local guitar factory. How would you like to join us there someday?" Gramps asks.

"Love it!" Nevin answers.

We pull into the driveway at Nevin's and notice that the moving truck is gone (and Chance is gone too).

"See you tomorrow," Nevin says.

"See you," I say, still smiling.

"Thanks, Mr. Joe," Nevin says.

"You're welcome, but call me Gramps!"

"Thanks, Gramps!"

Nevin was grinning from ear-to-ear.

8

What a Mess

I wake up and my first thought is of getting together with Nevin! I take a quick shower and throw down a few bites of cereal before leaving for Nevin's place. When I head to the basketball hoop, I see Dad standing over a pile of bike parts--my bike parts! I can't believe it. Dad is talking on the phone. I can tell he's talking to Gramps.

"I'll be right over," I hear Gramps say. Dad hangs up.

"It looks like someone isn't too happy with you," Dad says. "Do you know who did this?"

"It had to be Chance," I say.

"Chance? You never talk about him."

"Well, he's a 100% bully, so I try to avoid him," I say.

"What would cause him to do this?" Dad asks.

"I don't know. Maybe when he heard we were going fishing, he got jealous."

"Hmm...that makes a little sense," Dad concludes, "but why?"

At that very minute, Nevin and his dad walk up the driveway, holding a bent and broken bike wheel.

"You too?" Dad asks.

"Yup," Nevin and Nevin's dad say, in unison.

"I thought it was because I was the new kid," Nevin says.

"Nah, it's because Chance is a jerk," I say.

While we are still standing in the yard, talking about the bike incident, Gramps rolls into the driveway and parks his truck to join us.

"Oh boy, what a mess!" Gramps says, looking at the bike parts.

Gramps doesn't say much more than that, but he looks over every bent bike wheel while holding his coffee cup in his other hand. My dad takes pictures of my bike. Then, we walk over to Nevin's place and take pictures of his broken bike, too. It is upsetting to see Nevin's bike broken. It makes no sense. I guess just being my friend made Nevin a target. Dad, Paul (Nevin's dad), and Gramps talk longer and then they start walking down the driveway together. They are heading to Chance's house on the other side of Meadow Farms.

"What a way to start your first day in the new neighborhood," I say.

"Bullies are everywhere," Nevin says.

"Well, it's not okay what happened. It's not okay we have broken bikes, and Chance is probably going to act the same way at school," I say.

"I just hope we can get the bikes going again," Nevin says.

"My dad is pretty handy," I say. "Gramps can help us too."

"So what do you think is happening with Chance right now?"

"He's getting into huge trouble, I bet."

"I sort of want to know how much trouble, don't you?" Nevin asks.

"Actually, I do," I reply.

We both start to walk fast at the same second, and I guess we thought we could catch up with everyone. I feel a little funny sneaking around to see what kind of trouble Chance is in. Yet, it seems like it could be worth it, and I know Nevin wants to see what will happen next. Before my dad knocks on the door of Chance's home at 321 Sterling Heights, Nevin and I jump behind the hedgerow. We are in perfect earshot of the door.

"Good morning, Mrs. Theil," Grandpa Joe says.

"Good morning," Mrs. Theil replies.

"Hi, Mrs. Theil, my name is Paul and this is Andrew," Nevin's dad says, in a soft, gentle voice. "I'm new to Meadow Farms."

"Oh, I didn't realize but, *welcome*," Mrs. Theil says, cheerfully.

"Is Chance home?" Grandpa asks.

"No, actually he isn't, but is that why you're here?" she asks.

"Well, I'm afraid it is," Dad says.

"Please come in."

"Oh, thank you," both dads say, stepping into her home.

"Now what?" I ask, looking at Nevin.

"Let's just wait for a min--"

"What a lovely back yard," Dad's voice lifts over Mrs. Theil's backyard fence.

"Perfect, let's move closer," I say.

Nevin and I move to the side yard next to the fence and listen to our dads deliver the story of the damaged bike discovery to Chance's mom.

"Mrs. Theil," Gramps says.

"Call me Sheila."

"Sheila, the three of us believe we could offer you some support by spending time with Chance," he says.

"Well, I should tell you, it's been a tough road for him. Two years ago, when we were on vacation, his dad died of a heart attack.

To be more specific, it happened when Chance and his dad were on a remote trail riding their bikes. They didn't bring a cell phone and there was no way for Chance to get help, he tried giving his dad CPR, but he was only eight years old then. There was no way for him to get help, quickly. Finally, rangers were sent out on a search and they found Chance and my husband and you can imagine... Chance has never been the same," Sheila explains.

"Sheila, I'm very sorry," Paul says, with sadness in his voice.

"We would really like to help, maybe we could spend some time with Chance and step in a little here and there like a dad would, perhaps" Paul says.

"I have a workshop and I take the boys on outings from time to time," Gramps says, "I can easily invite Chance along," Gramps says.

"I would love to see Chance spending time with positive people," Shiela said.

"Well, the first thing we plan to do is take Chance into the workshop with us and fix a couple bikes."

"Perfect place to start," Sheila says, smiling. "I appreciate this, he has become hard toward others, and his cold heart is even tougher to reach than I know how to deal with," she adds, sadly.

"What time will Chance be home?" Gramps asks.

"Oh, I need to pick him up in about twenty minutes," she replies, glancing at her phone.

"Tae Kwon Do?" Paul asks.

"Yes," she says.

"I have thirteen years of martial arts training," Paul says.

"Really? Chance would respect that," Sheila replies.

"I think we all have something to offer Chance," Gramps says.

"Me too," she says, beaming with tears in her eyes.

"We might not be able to fix all everything, but at least we can remind Chance he's not alone, and people do care," Paul explains, reaching over to touch Sheila's arm.

"Sheila, Chance is going to be just fine," Dad says.

"Thank you, Paul," she replies.

They walk back through the house and I think there have to be five minutes of silence in the backyard before Nevin and I move an inch. We don't say anything until Sheila pulls her car out of the garage and leaves to pick-up Chance.

"I had no idea," I say.

"Who would have known?" Nevin says.

"I can't imagine finding my dad on the ground and trying to bring him back to life, out in the middle of nowhere, with only your bike!"

"What do you do--leave or stay and to help him?" Nevin asks.

"It sounds awful," I say.

"Sure does," he replies.

We walk home in silence. Everything about Chance and what he had done wrong sort of melts away. I feel like I need to rethink everything I felt about Chance up to now.

"If anyone can turn things around, it's my dad," Nevin says.

"Or my dad," I say.

"Or Gramps!" we say in unison, smiling at each other.

9

Moon Songs

My long awaited night is front and center and it's unfolding before my eyes! It feels like my mind is playing tricks on me. Am I dreaming? Gramps, Lindy, Nevin and I are sitting around the campfire at a campsite about twenty miles from Grandpa's and a short hike from Lake Michigan.

Even the mosquitoes are enjoying themselves. For some reason their bites don't bother me tonight. The moon is coming up full, orange, and I think it's the most fantastic night ever!

"Nevin, did you always live in New York?" Gramps asks.

"Yup, for as long as I can remember," he replies.

"What brought your family to Kalamazoo?" Gramps asks.

"My dad is a doctor. He's going to teach at the medical school."

"What kind of doctor?" Gramps asks.

"He's an oncologist."

"Oh how interesting. What do you think about Michigan?"

"I like it. I want to see more places, like I've only been to the beach once, and there are many places I want to go," Nevin says.

"Like where?" Gramps replies.

"First, I want to go with you to Gibson since you invited me. I want to meet the luthiers. I love guitars!" Nevin says.

"Well, that's an easy request. Next?"

"Next, I want to pick blueberries. I guess I missed the picking season this year, but I heard they have great fields of fruits around here, and blueberries are my favorite," Nevin says.

"We have a lot of 'pick-your-own' gardens. I would love to take you and Hunter to some of the farms and to the Kalamazoo Farmers' market," Gramp says.

"Do you want to play?" Gramp asks, looking at me and handing me the guitar.

"Gramps! I'm honored, yet... I would happier if you would play something for us, Nevin," I say, handing him Grandpa's Gibson.

Gramps smiles, "Go ahead, you only get a nickel in this life, play it."

"Okay," he replies, beaming.

Nevin accepts the Gibson Dove and starts strumming. Grandpa tells us the story of how he found his Gibson. As he is speaking, the strumming starts to turn into smooth sounding songs, and I can't believe what I hear Nevin playing on the strings! His songs sound sharp and then soft at exactly the right times when his hand hits the strings. My worries about not having a friend have lifted past the stars. I have no wishes left it seems. If a falling star would fall, I would let it drop for free. I can't think a bad thought, if I try. Sparks from the fire light the sky and fireflies dance against the trees. Nevin's easy strumming on the Dove makes this night impossible to forget. It's not just the best night since we moved to Kalamazoo, it's the best night ever! To my surprise, Nevin starts singing a song to the music. Somehow, I knew that moment, Nevin and I would be friends forever and that was that.

"So, where are we going tomorrow?" Gramps asks.

"Lake Michigan!" I blurt out.

"Sound good, Nevin?"

"Yup, sounds great," he says, tuning the guitar. "What should I bring?"

"Bring a towel and your swimsuit," Gramps says.

"I'll bring the rest, and Hunter, you're in charge of bringing a ball for the beach and a bottle of sunscreen. Okay?"

"Got it!" I say.

Over the next two weeks we went to Lake Michigan, and when we weren't with Gramps, Nevin and I pounded the downtown streets of Kalamazoo with my Mom. She shopped and read in the park while we found stops with stuff to do, and great food. We made our way into every place that seemed as we joked, "Kool-a-zoo." Gramps announced a few days ago, to Nevin and me, he was going to be busy on Saturdays for awhile. He explained he planned to spend time with Chance. He said we would have to find stuff to do or bug our moms to take us places. Nevin and I didn't mind. We were having fun just being together. It didn't seem to matter where we were having fun, as long as we had a ball or a guitar. Something great to eat was a bonus, but it didn't matter. Life was perfectly fine, as long as we were together.

Wolf Lake Fish Hatchery c. 1927

Wolf Lake Fish Hatchery Raceway

Matching small parts - Shakespeare Products Company 1936

Spinning Room - Shakespeare Products Company 1936

Reel Assembling - Shakespeare Products Company 1936
by Mamie L. Austin

10

A Chance with Gramps

"Hey, Hunter, come out here for a second please?" Dad asks.

"Okay, what's up?" I ask.

"You'll see. Please hurry." he says, sounding excited.

Outside of the house in the front of the garage Nevin, Gramps, Paul and Chance were waiting. "Okay, click it," Dad says.

Chance clicks the garage opener and two shiny bikes with new paint, clean lines of pin-stripping, perfect tires, and straightened-out handle bars are there. Four new lights, two shiny mirrors, and saddle bags have been added to both of them.

"Wow! They look better than they did before," I say.

"Not even a scratch--how did you do it?" Nevin asks.

"It was a team effort," Dad says, smiling at Chance.

"Everybody load up," Paul says.

"We're going for a ride!" Gramps says, glowing.

"All of us?" I ask.

"Yep, all of us, we're going to show off your new bikes on the Kal-Haven," Dad replies.

This is the biggest group ride I have been on. There is a feeling of excitement mixed with pure goodness in the air. In minutes, we're unloading our bikes in the parking lot at the 10th Street Kal-Haven trailhead.

After a long ride, filled with laughter and jokes, we land at *Klassic Arcade* in Gobles, Michigan. Our dads have lined up soda pop prizes for the pinball tournament, and there are thirty-some friends and family members waiting for us inside the arcade. Even Chance's mom came! My mom too, and Nevin's family. Everyone is finding their favorite game! Gramps watches Chance show off lightning fast Tae Kwon Do reflexes in a game of *Joust*! It's more fun going to the vintage arcade with our dads; since they grew up on these games. My dad and Paul are having a competitive match to see who can get the high score on *Centipede*.

We had sodas, played for a couple of hours, and then rode our bikes home. I'll never forget that day! Kalamazoo is getting bigger and brighter all of the time. At the *Air Zoo*, at the *Gilmore Car Museum*, and everywhere you look in the faces of people on Rose Street. I feel the city's spirit at the library and in the hands of those who serve at the Gospel Mission where Gramps took me, and Nevin and Chance to see how people care about each other. The spirit of Kalamazoo is making a good place inside of me, and makes me feel at home.

Six Months Later

11

Season Opener

As my eyes are opening to the morning sun, thoughts of a dream I had just experienced are fresh in my mind. In the dream, I was sailing on the *Friendship Goodwill*. My dream was a replay of a boat trip we took last fall with Dad, Chance and Nevin. I remember it clearly. We went last year over Labor Day, after we had a pancake breakfast at South Haven's Lions shelter. Dad's work had given him an easy fall schedule and the trip came as a surprise. Dad planned the trip for Chance, Nevin and me to go on the *Friendship Goodwill*. Chance had never been on a boat before, not even a canoe. Sailing on the waves of Lake Michigan was unforgettable. In my dream it was like yesterday. We were standing on the bow of the *Friendship Goodwill*. We were pulling on the mast ropes, and pretending to be sailors!

After we finished sailing we turned into pirates on the dunes. We ran up and down the sandy trails. We fought canibals on the beaches. We pretended we were shipwrecked. When my dad joined in, we started to play hide and seek. Just when we couldn't find Dad, he would jump up and chase us across the trails on the dunes. We ended up running and laughing a lot. Dad was pretty fast. He stayed right on our tails! In the end, we had to head for the lake and all three of us ran right into Lake Michigan. My dad didn't

stop there. He ran behind us! He didn't hesitate a second, laughing and chasing us, he landed in the water. He was wearing his sandals and clothes. It was hilarious! Or "hoo-larious" as Nevin always says! I could not contain myself that day, and dreaming about it, well, I guess it meant something deeper to me than I realized. It was a great dream!

Laying in bed, I start to think how fast time has clicked by me with Thanksgiving and winter holidays. Nevin, Chance and I are doing more things together. Chance has changed a lot. Chance and Gramps are spending Saturday mornings together and they've been doing this for months; since last September. Often, we will all go together. Chance seems like a completely different person. Over the winter months I learned most of the chords on guitar. Nevin and I have been going to the gym together after school. When we get to the gym, we go straight to the indoor batting cages. Nevin likes watching me instead of batting for himself. That's okay with me. In four days, my first Kalamazoo baseball season at Westwood Little League kicks-off. Gramps is working in the concession stand for my second game, and I want to make really good hits during our first game when he's there! There was a wild rumor going around the dugout that Derek Jeter had plans of making an appearance this year. Some people are saying that they heard he might be donating some new equipment to Westwood Little League. I won't believe my eyes, if Derek Jeter walks onto the mound! Just to see him in the stands at Westwood would knock my socks off! I can't wait for our first game. The toughest part is going to be falling asleep the night before. Who knows? Maybe Dered Jeter will show up! Coach Jake says I will be on first base, and then I will be on the mound as second-string pitcher. I have to stay focused or I could miss out.

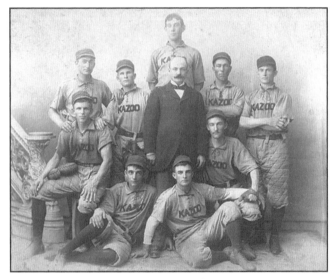

Kalamazoo baseball team, with manager
Oliver Guy Hungerford (standing center) c. 1886

12

Concessions

"What a hit!" Gramps says.

"I couldn't believe it," I reply.

"That had to feel good," he says.

"It did, and then when I rounded the turn I knew it would be close."

"You slid underneath the glove like a champ!" Gramps says.

"Hunter, I'll be back for the last inning, if I can get someone to cover for me," Gramps adds, walking toward the concession stand.

"No problem," I shout to him.

Gramps is king of the concession stand on Tuesdays. He organizes the parents on our team and they take turns handing out hot dogs, snow cones, and every kind of penny candy you can imagine. Gramps can usually work it out and gets back to the ballgame for a few minutes of the last inning. He usually shows up right after the last blast call for hot dogs. I love having Gramps at Little League. It's nice to have a sports family who takes turns and watches out for each other like the Westwood families do.

"Hunt, I'm going to need you on the mound," Coach Robbins says, walking by me.

"Sure," I say.

"Warm up on the side with Charlie, okay?" Coach says.

"Okay," I answer.

I love pitching, and I like when Charlie catches for me. He always seems to snag ones that fly out of the box, and that makes me feel better. I do not like the sound of balls hitting the back stop chain; it shakes my nerves a bit when I hear that awful sound, but Charlie has a great reach. I think he's catching for me next, or at least I hope so. We take 30 throws and they call the inning after Rudy strikes out. The crackle of the PA interrupts my thoughts on pitching.

"Attention: all Westwood families and players please stay in the stands and do not to come to the concessions," a voice says, calmly. "We have a medical emergency, and we need available nurses or doctors to report to the concession stand, immediately," the voice on the PA says.

The next thing I know, Paul, Nevin's dad, stands up and runs as fast I have ever seen him move. Something about seeing that just sank in the bottom of my stomach.

"Again, we ask everyone to please continue playing ball and refrain from coming to the concession stand. An ambulance is arriving in a few minutes. Do not block the parking area or attempt to drive from the parking lot until you hear *all clear*," a voice instructs.

I walk to the area of the stands were my parents are sitting.

"Do we keep playing?" I ask my Dad.

"Yes," he says.

Again, the sound of the PA loudspeaker clicks on.

"Mr. and Mrs. Andrew Dale," please come to the concession stand," the voice says.

"Stay here, Hunter," Dad says.

"It's Gramps," I say. "Please, Dad, I need to..."

"Okay, come with," he says, looking concerned.

We run toward the concession stand. I see the ambulance moving in, and a circle of people forming around the medical team. I see the paramedics going to the concession stand with a stretcher. Next, I see them lift Gramps onto the stretcher. I'm scared now. I see Paul get in the ambulance. My mom is there and she is getting into the ambulance with my grandpa. My dad looks at me and at the ambulance. He must know I'm afraid Gramps won't make it.

"We will meet them at the hospital," he says.

In my mind, my thoughts are rushing. Surreal is the best word to describe my feeling. I feel helpless too. I keep thinking about Gramps putting his hand on my shoulder, right after I hit the home run and slid into the plate. Now it seems a bittersweet victory with the calls across the loud speaker, and the ambulance taking Grandpa to the hospital.

Grandpa Joe had suffered a massive heart attack. He could have died on the way the hospital but, he didn't die that day. At the hospital Gramps was put into intensive care, and two emergency surgeries followed. Things changed from minute-to-minute. We waited in small lobbies and kept each other company. Grandma had been crying and we knew our lives would never be the same without Gramps, if he didn't make it. Thankfully, he survived.

Peace Pagent at Frank Street School, Kalamazoo, Michigan 1915

13

War and Peace

A lot of things changed after Gramps had a heart attack. First, I noticed Grandma Ann and Mom started taking over things Grandpa normally did himself. Even some of his volunteer activities. Mom could have called the places where Gramps volunteered and said he couldn't help for medical reasons. Instead Mom volunteered in his place. She and Grandma made a number of calls and meetings to continue where Gramps left off, volunteering. Two weeks to the day that Gramps went to the hospital there was a community event happening. The Volunteer Center called and gave my mom some names of other people who wanted to help; since they knew my grandpa and what had happened.

The event, called *Peace Pizzazz,* is scheduled for May 17th at Bronson Park. Gramps had been planning to play guitar for them. Gramps and some of the Heritage luthiers went to Peace Pizzazz; since they were fond of helping out where they could with local parades and festivals.

"Grandpa had been helping to plan Peace Pizzazz and now he's going to have to watch, heal and make some changes to take better care of himself," Mom says.

In light of Gramps needing time to mend, Grandma asks Mom to help put finishing touches on Peace Pizzazz and to manage a few event activities.

In light of Gramps needing time to mend, Grandma asks Mom to help put finishing touches on Peace Pizzazz and to manage a few event activities.

"If I had not had a chance to help with Peace Pizzazz I would not have realized how much Grandpa Joe believed in initiating displays of kindness," Mom explains.

"Your Grandpa is a work of art, as far as humans go, he always supports the military, and especially the Army. He served during Vietnam you know, Hunter," Mom explains. "Yet, he helped promote peaceful living, too."

"Grandma, did he ever tell you about his time in war or anything about what he saw there?" I ask.

"No, Gramps doesn't talk about Vietnam often, but frequently he says he's proud he served his country in the military," Grandma replies. "I think for him, it's too tough to remember those scary times. When he first came home from Vietnam, he told me once, even though he didn't want to, he finally had to see a counselor to talk about and try to overcome fears attached to harsh memories of war.

"He remembers many good folks dying in Vietnam," she explains. "Your grandpa believes people need to try harder in this age to live in peace."

"It sounds like his memories could be tough to bear," I say.

"When he's feeling a little better, maybe he would like to tell you about his thoughts on peace and war. As a vet, it's best when countries get along with each other, and avoid war whenever possible," Grandma explains.

"I remember Gramps feeling sad the year 9/11 happened. Mom says.

"So this is why Gramps is part of the group that organized" *Peace Pizzazz?*"

After 9/11 Gramps felt America had no choice. He felt, like many, our country had to fight terrorism.

"Gramps would tell you, there are no easy answers when senseless acts of violence happen," Grandma adds.

"I'm not glad Grandpa had a heart attack but it helped to get me more involved in projects. As his daughter, it's nice to build peace in our city like Dad has been doing for many years," Mom says. "He has a vision of the world, treating one human at a time with tolerance and kindness to keep our freedoms strong and our USA solid as it ever was."

"Wow, I had no idea Gramps was such a believer in peace. I thought he was really into soldiers and war, since he hung out with his veteran friends."

"Gramps has always felt soldiers were amazing servants, and not just war vets but kids today, who voluntarily put themselves at risk in the military," Mom explains.

"If you get Gramps going on this topic, he'll tell you, most soldiers are peace-loving," Grandma adds. "Soldiers hold the bill of sacrifice, and most probably feel war is no place to be."

"What are we going to do exactly at *Peace Pizzazz?*"

"Well, Gramps organized some of the Heritage guys to work at a table to make handmade instruments, some are making canjos. Canjos are small banjos made from a piece of wood and a soup can. Others are cutting plastic guitar picks from old CD's," Mom says.

"Your grandpa should be feeling much better by Peace Pizzazz and he's going to make canjos with his friends!"

Popcorn Wagon in Bronson Park Kalamazoo, MI 1947
by Elizabeth Johnson

14

Unopened

After dinner that night, Grandma Ann tells Haylee that she wants to see if Zumi can come over for a few minutes.

"Gramps has something he wants to give to Zumi," Grandma explains.

"Okay, I'll go over to her place and see if she can come over," Haylee says.

About twenty minutes later, Grandma, Grandpa, Zumi and Haylee are sitting together at the kitchen table. Gramps looks much better now than he did in the hospital. There's a happy feeling in the room and when Gramps takes out a shopping bag with a small gift box.

"Zumi, this is for you," Grandpa says.

"It has been sitting on my workshop table and I wanted to give it to you for your birthday but with my heart problems, I sort of forgot until this week when I went back into my shop," Grandpa says.

"For me?" Zumi asks.

"For you," Gramps replies.

Zumi opens the box to find a necklace. Zumi shows it around and passes it to Haylee for her to see it too. It's a square, glass pendant made with a painting of trees neatly sealed behind a thin, smooth piece of glass.

"You really made this for me?" Zumi asks.

"I really did," Gramps says.

"I started making necklaces for people, after taking a class on glass blowing and working with tile and metal fittings such as these," he explains, pointing to the necklace in Zumi's hand.

You can tell Zumi loves the necklace. Grandma Ann drapes it around her neck and Grandpa looks content. I'm so glad it wasn't Grandpa's time to die and that his doctors and nurses are helping him address his heart problems. Watching Zumi put on her necklace reminds me of how many people Gramps cares about and does nice things for, in his life. In the days after he returned from the hospital, cards and letters were pouring into their home. Since that day, life has been very different for him. One way it's been different is not seeing Chance come outside his house. I'm guessing Gramps having a heart attack gave Chance a big shock; since he lost his dad to a heart attack and probably struggled with this more than others.

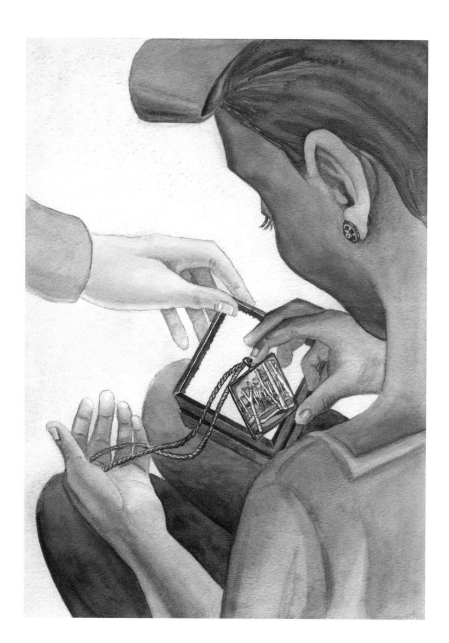

Downtown Kalamazoo, Michigan 1983 by Perry C. Riddle.

15

Peace in the Backyard

Knock-Knock-Knock

"Good morning Mrs. Theil," I say.

"Good morning Hunter." she replies.

"Is Chance here?"

"Yes, let me get him for you."

"Hey Chance," I say.

"How's it going, Hunter?" he asks.

"Pretty good," I reply. "How would you like to go with us today?"

"Where?" he asks.

"*Peace Pizzazz* at Bronson Park," I say.

"Hmm, what is that?"

"It's a big festival where everyone celebrates peace, and they have music and food, and stuff like that," I say.

"How's is Gramps?" Chance asks.

"He's doing great," I reply.

"Really," Chance says, brightening up. "Will he be going to Peace Pizzazz too?"

"Yup, we're all going!"

"Okay, Mommmm," Chance yells. "I'm going with Hunter."

"Be back by dinner," she replies.

Dad puts his hand on Chance's shoulder.

"How have you been since Gramps hasn't been around?"

"I'm okay, but I'm still feeling scared to see Gramps," Chance says.

"Why?"

"I keep thinking Gramps will die just like my dad did," he says.

I see the tears start pouring down Chance's face. I can't hold back my tears, I cried too, just seeing him cry.

"When Gramps had his heart attack I was sure Gramps would die too," I say.

"He didn't though, and we were all scared, but not every life event or medical emergency has to end sadly," he says.

"I was sure it would," Chance says.

"Did you learn anything about yourself during all of this?"

"I want to be like Gramps; especially when he's not around anymore. I want to be someone who pitches in and cares for people," Chance says.

"Chance, you have a lot of good in you, and Gramps more than anyone knows that. You have to believe what he told you. Even though he's adjusting he'll come back and be part of our lives again," Dad says. "Gramps cares about you and so do others," he adds, looking right at Chance.

"I know, but no one cared about me like Gramps," Chance says.

"No, but we need to find the good in others like Gramps does, and keep an open mind. You can be a person that fills the gap," Dad says.

"It seems like I'm angry when I think about losing Gramps." Chance says.

"Dying is part of life, and it can be a really tough part," Dad says. "We all have one life, one nickel to play and we have to find the best way to spend every minute we have on earth."

"Let's give your mom a call. We have a date in Bronson Park today with Gramps and Chance, you should be there with us," Dad says.

"Maybe your mom could come too," Nevin says.

"That's a great idea," Dad agrees.

"Lindy too?"

"Of course!"

"Bring Lindy's dawg stick to Bronson too. Your gramps would like to see her fetching a stick, I bet!"

"Sure, let's toss a few in the yard for her before we take off," he answers.

Chance throws the stick in the yard. With each throw of the stick a ball of stress goes flying in the air. The wriggly body of Lindy returns the stick to us. Chance gently pulls the stick from her mouth, and tosses it into the air again for her. With each toss of the stick a smile appears on Chance's face, and every minute seems lighter. Gramps will be okay, and Chance will grow from withstanding a heavy fear of losing him. The day is improving. *Peace Pizzazz* started before we even arrived with the friendship that grew from the backyard conversation with Chance.

16
Pizzazz at the Park

We arrive in downtown Kalamazoo and it looks like 500 people are strolling around Bronson Park. *Peace Pizzazz* is alive with colorful flags, balloons and music floating over the crowd like a rabble of butterflies. Bronson Park attracts people from nearby downtown shops and restaurants. From every direction people flow into the park on Bronson's swerving sidewalks. Kids are playing in the park's dry fountain bed, and a few kids are running around a grassy hillside while others are sitting on blankets. In different places around the park, bands of peacemakers are crafting, chatting, and listening to music. Families are visiting the tables and booths where different people have displays about peace, kindness, and other friendly messages. A small band pounds out songs from the center of Rotary Stage. A big sign hangs from the stage. *These musicians stick to peace like flies!* The band is called *Fly Paper,* and the lead singer is an attractive women with long, raven hair. The singer plays a guitar too, but I can't tell if it's a Gibson or some other kind of guitar. Her voice is belting salty lyrics across the park. The first person we see is a sight for sore eyes: Gramps!

Gramps spots us at about the same exact time we see him. It is a great way of seeing him after visits in the hospital or at home where he often has been resting. It is great to see Gramps on his

feet. I love seeing him against the backdrop of *Peace Pizazz* with summer vibrations going airborne and people celebrating. Gramps is beaming at us as he walks our way.

"Hey Chance!"

"Gramps," Chance says, giving him a handshake.

"Come here," he says, hugging Chance. "Good to see you."

"You too, really good to see you!" Chance says, smiling.

"Hey Gramps," I say.

"Hunter, is that your school helping at the canjo table?"

"Yup, it's my teacher and some of my friends," I reply.

"This is the biggest *Peace Pizzazz* I've been to so far!"

"Next year will probably be even better," I reply, smiling.

"You're right, *Peace Pizzazz* keeps growing every single year."

17

Healing on the Horizon

Often Dad invites Chance, Lindy or Nevin, and we go out to South Haven to fly kites. This Saturday, it is just Dad and me. We take our time on the beach and we watch the boats and people under their umbrellas.

"Hunter, I think I'll make a 'food run' for us, maybe grab a bag of burgers so we can enjoy the sunset here," Dad says.

"Sounds good," I reply, pulling out my guitar pick, and positioning my guitar to play some songs on the pier.

The idea of learning to play guitar, like Gramps settles somewhere deep inside of me. Learning to play guitar, can be one way that I will always remember Gramps, and his voice, singing or his Dove strumming along to a song. Someday I know Gramps will die. For now, I have to appreciate gaining a little more time on earth with him.

I watch the end of the sunset at South Haven. I feel that a chapter is turning in my life. I feel like the sunsets in Ohio were nothing like the one in front of me, on the horizon of Lake Michigan. Oddly, I feel comfort in thinking about my home in Kalamazoo.

Dad's hand lands on my shoulder.

"Whatcha thinkin" Dad asks.

"Gramps always told me, a great song tells a story, I'm thinking that I might not make this guitar famous like Lucy, but I could make Gramps proud."

"I was just thinking about a song line," I reply.

I start singing, "South Haven sunset takes up the darkness in July..."

Strumming against the Gibson Dove, my fingers feel more alive than they have in awhile. Gramps would be proud, if I can sing a couple songs to keep his favorite tunes alive.

Dad chimes in, and sings with me. The feelings of Kalamazoo as my new home and Gramps being alive fills my heart with thankfulness and song.

The fear of never having friends is gone. The thoughts I had of Ohio were crossing over the water of South Haven and getting lost in pink tangerine over a faintly dappled starlit sky.

Credits

This book was made possible by the following organizations and individuals and from their archival collections:

Jessie Fales at Epic Fales Photography

Everyone at the Heritage Guitar Company

Patrick Jouppi and staff members of the Local History Center, at the Kalamazoo Public Library

Arcadia, Prairie Ridge, King-Westwood and Washington Elementary Schools; also, Linden Grove Middle School of Kalamazoo Public Schools

Jeters Leaders - Derek Jeter & the Turn 2 Foundation

Paula Metzner at Kalamazoo River Valley Museum

Peace Pizzazz & Peace Jam

Paw Paw Public Library

Michigan Department of Natural Resources

Westwood Little League

Wolf Lake Fish Hatchery Staff Members

Special Acknowledgements
Luthiers of Inspiration in the Gibson World

Two notable luthiers inspired the character named Ren. First, Rendall Wall - born 1942. Ren worked at Gibson Guitar Company from 1960-1982. Ren Wall provided the main inspiration for one of the characters in this book. Ren, a fine craftsman developed several guitars and engineered many models for famous musicians over the years. Ren tells his luthier stories, freely and without hesitation. Ren's exceptional oral history has been recorded by Kalamazoo River Valley Museum and can be found under the Ren Wall History Project. The online recording is a valuable treasure of Ren's interesting collection of memories. His personal account captures fascinating aspects of what he has done through the years in the guitar building business. Ren has continued to make guitars and has produced exceptional guitars in the same building, now called Heritage Guitars. Listening to Ren is touching a real-life artisan who shaped American history.

Secondly, a talented Gibson luthier, Ren Ferguson headed a small team in Bozeman, Montana. The roots of Gibson started in Kalamazoo. Ren Ferguson's story as a Gibson luthier can be reviewed by going on-line and searching the archives of Gibson history, the account of Ren Ferguson's influence is called "Made by Hand: The Story of Gibson Acoustic," an article written by Dave Hunter. Special thanks to both "Rens" for dedication to the craft and for those who are working to share and preserve their stories. Ren Wall: "Your willingness and openness drew us deeper into the Gibson story; since your tales will continually inspire us to share Gibson history with young readers around the world!"

Internet Discussion Points

Use each word to research interesting topics. Start key word searches with your child and see what you can lean with them online.

Archtop (guitar term)

Blues & Bluegrass

Culture

Fish Hatchery

Flattop (guitar term)

Heritage

Luthier

Oncologist

Peace Movement

Pythagorean Expectation

Raceway (aquaculture)

Rock & Rockabilly

Shakespeare Fishing Equipment 1896

Square Topsail Sloop

Terrorism

Hunter's Top Picks
Books for Young Readers

Brave Girl: Clara and the Shirtwaist Makers Strike of 1909
by Michelle Markel

From Kalamazoo to Timbucktu! by Harriet Ziefert

Granddad's Fishing Buddy by Mary Quigley

I Went to the Party in Kalamazoo
by Ed Shankman & Dave Frank

Kalamazoo Long Ago by Grace J. Potts
(out of print copies are available)

Peace by Wendy Anderson Halperin

The Juice Box Bully by Bob Sornson & Maria Dismondy

Trout, Trout, Trout by April Pulley Sayre

CD's for All

Dream by Fly Paper

Lucky Lindy by Steve Barber

Thumb Thump by Joel Mabus

Tone Poems by Tony Rice & David Grisman

Books for Moms & Dads and Older Folks

Grandparents Michigan Style by Mike Link & Kate Crowley

Guitar - An American Life by Tim Brookes

Kalamazoo Gals by John Thomas

Kalamazoo Lost & Found
by Lynn Smith Houghton, Pamela O'Connor &
Kalamazoo Historic Preservation Commission

Peace Jam: A Billion Acts of Peace
by Ivan Suvanjieff and Dawn Gifford Engle

Picks! by Will Hoover

War and Peace by Leo Tolstoy

Websites

www.artofmanliness.com
"So You Want My Job"
A section for parents and teachers to lead discussions about
different careers, includes luthiery.

www.lurelore.com
A resource hub for the fishing lure collector.

www.acousticmusic.org
History of guitar builders and all fretted instruments

www.historyprize.org
Describes the creative platform of the catalyst event being
developed around history.

Mara Mae
Author

Mara Mae lives with two of her three children on the Gogebic Iron Range where she supports the development of enriching the lives of people living at Michigan's Historic Gateway through the arts, heritage, and cultural experiences. Mara is an award-winning Michigan writer and founder of HISTORY PRIZE*. She is a member of the Michigan Historical Society, the Marquette Regional History Center, Ironwood Area Historical Society, Iron County Historical Society. Mara believes in creative place making and small business; also, buying local as much as possible. Her favorite places to spend time are in the woods, by the water and watching baseball games. She likes the wild ricing community and wishes every person in the Midwest could have a chance to harvest manoomin with a group of Native American people. *See websites for more information.

Dan Smith
Illustrator

Dan lives in Paw Paw, Michigan with his wife Laura. He is a consummate, watercolor artist who has been painting images of friends and family for many years. Dan is a retired elementary school principal and he enjoys spending time with his two sons and his granddaughter, Chelsea.

True Kazoo Foods

"Tell me what you eat, and I'll tell you who you are," wrote renowned gastronome Jean Anthelme Brillat-Savarin in 1825.

One way to learn about a group of people living in an area, is to see how they prepare, serve and celebrate food in their community. True Kazoo Foods, provides a glimpse of these "foodie" connections which often reflect readily available fresh vegetables and fruits and the diverse ethnicity of people living in Kalamazoo.

True Kazoo Foods discovers the historical backdrop of many regional restaurants along with those people who are making a difference in the lives of others. Along with Kalamazoo events like Art Hop and Rib Fest many Southwest Michigan restaurants shape the Kalamazoo food experience and improve the quality of life for visitors and locals.

Bimbo's Pizza is a part of Kalamazoo history and maintains their  spot in the area's Pizza Hall of Fame with the Bimbo's Pizza infamous claim "A treat in Michigan smuggled out of Italy!" Located in the heart of historic downtown Kalamazoo, Bimbo's Pizza gives visitors the feeling that they've stepped back in time by maintaining the 1880's architecture of the building. Bimbo's Pizza has been operating in this same location since 1959. Bimbo's Pizza shares the culture of the region by preserving their place in history, and by offering the Author's favorite: Bimbo's Pizza Special!

338 E. Michigan Ave., Kalamazoo, MI 49007   269-349-3134

Brewster's at the Dyckman

has roots in Paw Paw dating back to the late 1800's. The original purpose of the building was as a hotel, but the present day configuration is a restaurant/bar and apartment building. Brewster's at the Dyckman sits right on the corner of Michigan Avenue and Kalamazoo Avenue in downtown Paw Paw. It's impossible to miss as you're making your way through town. There is street parking in front and on the side

Early Dyckman House building Paw Paw, MI

of the building, but there's also a municipal parking lot around back which serves all the businesses along this busy stretch of road. The large Brewster's menu selection includes vegetarian options and the atmosphere in the dining room has a casual and friendly feeling. Local historic photos provide a nice walk down Paw Paw's memory lane.

Hunter's Favorite: Reuben Sandwich — Author's Favorite: Fried Asparagus

201 E. Michigan Avenue, Paw Paw, MI 49079,   269-655-2222

Cancun Mexican Restaurant

The pleasant atmosphere boasts warm and friendly wait staff. The menu backs some of the most authentic Mexican food in the Kalamazoo area. The guacamole and chips are excellent; also the salsa is served generously and fresh. Cancun lunch specials are tough to beat on price and quality. Hunter's Choice: Wet Steak Burrito — Author's Choice: Carne a la Tampiquena

Vintage Street Scene in Paw Paw, MI

37908 Red Arrow Highway, Paw Paw, MI 49079   269-657-0107

CHINN•CHINN

AN ASIAN BISTRO

Lines at the door are not uncommon and the wait is certain to play out with crowd-pleasing dishes as Chinn Chinn is worth the wait. Chinn Chinn offers one of the best Chinese dining experiences in the region with what is often described as 5-star Asian gourmet. Haylee's Choice: Spring Rolls — Author's Favorite: Curry

52885 N. Main St., Mattawan, MI 49071   269-668-7667

This historic Michigan diner type has been offering the taste of Coney dogs for Kalamazonians since 1915. Coney Island is a tasty detour from the glossy menus of modern, American fast-food. Coney dogs can be traced back to the early 20th century. The 'Coney Dog' originated in Michigan. For Kalamazoo, the simplicity of a hot dog with fries is held to the highest standard of any competing Coney Dogs around the region. Hunter's Favorite: Cheese Fries — Gramp's Favorite: New York Coney Dog

266 E. Michigan Ave., Kalamazoo, MI 49007   269-382-0377

Confections with Convictions *Handcrafted with fair trade organic chocolate*

Confections with Convictions is the newest addition to the gourmet food scene in Kalamazoo Michigan. We specialize in truffles hand crafted with fair trade organic chocolate from original recipes by chocolatier Dale Anderson. We also stock organic, gourmet and fair trade chocolates from around the world. Confections with Convictions is located next to the Victorian Bakery.

Dale Anderson, chocolatier and founder of Confections with Convictions, has worked as a counselor with young people in the court system for several years. Through this work it became clear that talk therapy—while helpful—was often not enough to overcome the many barriers they face. Dale wanted to develop a more powerful way to help them become successful members of society.

After buying a box of artisan chocolates, he joked that maybe he should open a chocolate shop instead—and call it Confections with Convictions. The joke reflected the fact that he intended to hire youth with criminal records, as well as his desire to incorporate socially responsible principles into his business.

The idea stuck with him, and a few months later he became convinced that it had potential. Many of the youth are kinesthetic learners—ones who learn by doing. "The work would help them learn work and life skills on a job they are paid to do. We'd use only wholesome ingredients and sustainable business practices."

Dale spent three years studying and practicing the art of making fine chocolates, and then put his construction skills to work renovating a building for his shop on Crosstown Parkway in Kalamazoo. Confections with Convictions is now open, sharing the building with another artisanal shop, The Victorian Bakery. Stop by to see Dale's inspiration put into action producing fine artisanal chocolates and fine young citizens. Hunter's Truffle: Peanut Butter & Honey Author's Truffle: Walnut Maple Cranberry

116 W. Crosstown Pkwy., Ste. 101, Kalamazoo, MI 49001   269-381-9700

For nearly 20 years, **Food Dance** has been committed to building a thriving and sustainable local food system. We support artisans who practice craft food processes that have been around for generations—growing, raising, preserving, curing, aging, pickling, butchering and more. For Food Dance, it's about the connection with the people and places their food comes from—authentic people and authentic food that's true to its source. Serving breakfast, lunch or dinner–guests are served the freshest menu items in a casual and welcoming atmosphere. We offer private dining space for celebrations or larger groups as well as catering and delivery. We host cooking classes and special dinners throughout the year — aimed to introduce guests to new elements of the culinary and agricultural worlds. Our on-site market offers amazing ingredients sourced from their family of purveyors–from sustainable, humanely raised meats, sausages and artisan cheeses to fresh baked bread, pastries and savory baked goods.

Haylee's Favorite: Classic Macaroni and Cheese — Author's Favorite: Winter Squash Risotto

401 E. Michigan Ave. #100, Kalamazoo, MI 49007   269-382-1888

Four Roses Cafe is a casual, fine dining cafe in Plainwell, Michigan. Our focus is on fresh, flavorful dishes and outstanding service. Our menu changes daily and will be determined by what is available in local markets each day. Chef/Owner Tom Rose believes dining out should be a memorable experience. His culinary team creates dishes that will excite your palate and have you looking forward to your next visit and anticipating what the new features will be. Four Roses Cafe's menu has many well known favorites such as Fresh Whitefish Grenoble and Roasted Pork Loin, and  is adding new dishes such as Maple Mustard Baby Back Ribs and Stuffed Lamb daily. The tradition of great desserts in Plainwell also continues at Four Roses. Kris Newland is in the pastry kitchen creating favorites like Peanut Butter Pie, Black Bottom Pie and Sticky Toffee Pudding as well as many seasonal fruit desserts.

Hunter's Favorite: BBQ Chicken Quesadilla — Favorite: Filet Mignon w/Béarnaise Sauce

663 10th Street, Plainwell, MI 49080   269-685-1077

Fruit growers in Southwest Michigan

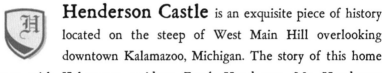 **Henderson Castle** is an exquisite piece of history located on the steep of West Main Hill overlooking downtown Kalamazoo, Michigan. The story of this home began with Kalamazoo resident, Frank Henderson. Mr. Henderson was one of early Kalamazoo's most successful businessmen. He was the

owner and president of the Henderson-Ames Company which made uniform regalia for secret societies, fraternal organizations, and the military. The Queen Anne style house was designed by C. A. Gombert of Milwaukee, Wisconsin. The $72,000 building costs included seven baths (one with a thirteen-head shower), an elevator, and a third-floor ballroom. The castle's exterior was constructed of Lake Superior sandstone and brick, and the interior wood included mahogany, bird's eye maple, quartered oak, birch, and American sycamore. The Henderson's had a grand housewarming party in 1895 at the completion of the castle's construction. Mr. Henderson died in 1899 and his wife remained at the castle until 1908. After Mrs. Henderson moved away, nine parties have owned Henderson Castle. In 1957 the house was purchased as the future site for the Kalamazoo Art Center. However, when the Institute of Arts remained downtown Kalamazoo, the castle became the property of the renowned liberal arts school at Kalamazoo College which lies just a block to the north of the castle's grounds.

Mom's Favorite: Steak Diane —— Gramps's Favorite: Steamed Flounder

100 Monroe St., Kalamazoo, MI, 49006   269-344-1827

Just Good Food is located in the Rose Street Market. Exceptional catering for wedding receptions, corporate events, private parties or any special occasion. Serving breakfast, lunch, dinner and appetizers, cooked "from scratch" using local, organic, fresh ingredients. Casual dining and a true Kalamazoo hidden treasure.

Haylee's Pick: You Gotta Have It Sandwich

Author's Favorite: Marinated Strawberries

   303 N. Rose St., Kalamazoo, MI 49007   269-383-1033

Olde Peninsula Brewpub and Restaurant, Kalamazoo's

first brewpub was originally designed for the Peninsula Restaurant. Previously, Olde Peninsula has been a book binding and printing company, a clothing store, hotel, Kalamazoo stove company and became the W.R. Biggs/Gilmore Agency in 1973. The three story structure was built by Nicholas Bowman in 1874 and one point suffered damage by the 1980 tornado. The building was completely rehabilitated in 1981.

Olde Peninsula Brewpub and Restaurant hosts a relaxing atmosphere, friendly staff, hand crafted ales, and large menu selection. The menu features everything from salads and burgers to pasta and steaks. In addition to the regular menu and five permanent tapped beers are featured on rotating seasonal menu. Open for lunch and dinner seven days a week, Olde Peninsula is the perfect place for your business luncheon, relaxing dinner with family or friends, or any special event! Everybody's Favorite: Brewpub Pot Roast

   200 E. Michigan Ave., Kalamazoo, MI 49007   269-389-0800

Rustica specializes in rustic European cuisine using local farmers and vendors whenever possible. With an emphasis on fresh, sustainable and

local products, Rustica blends influences from France, Italy, Spain and other European countries with regional Michigan fare. The food at Rustica is simple, fresh, and delicious.

Chef de Cuisine Chris Kidd and his Assistant Chef de Cuisine Scott Shattuck are both graduates of The Culinary Institute of America (CIA) in Hyde Park, NY. Their classical training is clearly reflected in the wide ranging disciplines and food styles executed at Rustica. House-cured meats, hand-made cheese, stocks, soups, and desserts are just some of the specialties that make dining at Rustica special. Rustica offers features on Friday and Saturday to compliment our regular ala carte menu. If you are a true foodie...Rustica will soon be your restaurant of choice. Haylee's Pick: Hand-Made Ricotta Gnocchi Mom's Favorite: Pan-Roasted Michigan Chicken

236 S. Kalamazoo Mall, Kalamazoo, MI 49007   269-492-0247

Shawarma King The best falafel from Lake Michigan to New York City. Shawarma King serves authentic middle eastern food at affordable prices. The quality and quantity are impossible to beat and happy Shawarma customers agree, you're sure to return again and again!

Your trip is likely to include kind-hearted treatment and warmth from a friendly staff. Hunter's Pick: Chicken Shawarma with pickles

Dad's Pick: King Combo

2925 S. Westnedge Ave., Kalamazoo, MI 49008   269-226-9700

The Victorian Bakery was started in the basement of a Victorian House, built in 1859 by a fellow Irishman. We were bringing baked goods to our son's schools as a treat for the teachers and they became so popular, we had future customers asking to buy scones and cakes. In December 2010, we moved the bakery to 116 W. Crosstown Parkway in Kalamazoo. What fun it is to be beside a chocolate shop! The Bakery uses flour from King Milling in Lowell, Michigan. The  pastry flour is grown and milled in Augusta, Michigan, and the vanilla used is made right here in Kalamazoo by National Flavors.

Hunter's Favorite: Millionaire's Shortbread

Gramp's Pick: Tart Michigan Cherry Scone

116 W. Crosstown Pkwy., Kalamazoo, MI 49001   269-553-6194

Zeb's Trading Company The atmosphere at Zeb's is warm and inviting. The dining area is an easy-going after work stop for many local residents and boasts a casual menu of steaks, burgers, chicken, and gluten-free items.   Nevin's Pick: Onion Rings Author's Pick: Prime Rib Sandwich

7990 S. 8th St., Kalamazoo, MI 49009   269-375-6778

Shakespeare's Pub

This is one of the actual buildings used by the Shakespeare Company where the Shakespeare rod and reels and other products were made. Now a restaurant, Shakespeare's Pub keeps the history of live with several photos of the original company on the walls of the establishment. Shakespeare Company started in 1897 in Kalamazoo and they have continued to create fishing equipment at affordable prices for families to experience nature and one of America's oldest pastimes. The building has a wonderful Art Deco style which serves as a distinguished reminder of the historic and iconic rod and reel company. Local musicians are known to play at Shakespeare's Pub and it is likely a few Gibson guitars have entered the building.

Author and Illustrator shared Shakespeare's favorite: Veggie Pizza

241 E. Kalamazoo Ave., Kalamazoo, MI 49007   269-488-7782

Shakespeare Company Inspection Room by Mamie L. Austin 1936

HARRISON PACKING CO., INC.
Institutional Pickle Packers Since 1939

Harrison Packing Company is the featured historical business that has been packing pickles since 1939. The enterprising family business carries a full line of pickle and pepper products.

Harrison offers institutional size containers: 4-1 gallon jars, 2 gallon pails, 5 gallon pails, and bulk drums. Harrison has a 250 piece minimum and delivers mainly in Chicago and Detroit. Harrison Packing is family owned and operated; Harrison Pickle Packing is currently on their fourth generation of Harrison's involved in the company. "Ma Harrison," one of the second

Ma Harrison performs a pickle qualtiy check.

generation, is still very involved with the company. At the age of 94, she is sharp as a tack, and keeps the rest of the company on their toes. The Harrison Packing Company delivers trailer load lots of 40,000 lbs. in pickles anywhere within the U.S.A. If

Harrison Packing Co. process approximately 200,000 bushels each year.

given the opportunity to stop over for a Wednesday pickle pick-up.

3420 Stadium Park Way, Kalamazoo, MI 49009   269-381-3837

HISTORY CPR
"Cultivate-Preserve-READ!"

the book series, invites children in public, private and homeschool settings to engage in developing stories around history, art and nature. Each History CPR book brings "History to Life" and allows readers to interact with authors in classrooms or on-line. Kids become creative partners with the author through interactive learning experiences that weave a fictional story with threads of real American history. Thousands of young readers helped the author create Hunter's Quest. Kids and families picked six handcrafted items which can be found in the illustrated pages of this book. Also, readers chose Michigan illustrator Dan Smith who, with diligent care, painted the images for this story.

Featured American Handcrafted Items and Artists:

Name / Art Studio	Item	Page
Rachel Linquist Hen And Chick	Dolls	21
Kathy Johnson The Bronze Flower	Bracelet	21
Benjamin Argall Blue Mohawk Studios	Necklace	67
Scott Snow Michigan in Metal	Clock	27
Linda The Hickory Tree	Dog Toy	72

Product Order Form

PHONE
906-235-0470

EMAIL
info@historyprize.org

WEB
historyprize.org

To order art pieces featured in the pages of Hunter's Quest or to order books in the History CPR book series please complete and mail this order form. Include your check or money order:

Old Wood Press
P. O. Box 777
Ironwood, MI 49938

DESCRIPTION	QUANTITY	UNIT PRICE	COST
Hunter's Quest #2		$ 15.95	
Great Lakes Clock		$ 69.95	
Haylee Doll		$ 59.95	
Zumi Doll		$ 59.95	
Image Your Quest - Copper Bracelet		$ 49.95	
Zumi's Michigan Trees Pendant & Necklace		$ 29.95	
Lindy Dawg Stick "personalized" for pooches		$ 19,95	
Lucky Lindy CD		$ 15.95	
Haylee's Treasure 2nd Edition (Avail. Dec 2015)		$ 15.95	
		Subtotal	$ 0.00
		Tax 6.00%	$ 0.00
		Total	**$ 0.00**

Credit card orders can only be processed on-line.

SHIP TO:

Your Name:_____

Address:_____

Address:_____

City:_____State:_____Zip:_____

Telephone #: _____

Scholarship benefits are based on years attending. Hunter coming to Kalamazoo in 3rd grade would actually receive "most" of his tuition; based on years attended:

Years Attended	Scholarship
K-12	100%
1-12	95%
2-12	95%
3-12	95%
4-12	90%
5-12	85%
6-12	80%
7-12	75%
8-12	70%
9-12	65%
10-12	None
11-12	None
12-12	None

The Kalamazoo Promise

- Work hard in school
- Graduate
- Earn a Promise scholarship
- Be successful in life

To learn details about the
Kalamazoo Promise
visit: kalamazoopromise.com